A Barbecue For Charlotte

by Marc Tetro

Many thanks to François Albert, who as usual comes to rescue me at the last minute. Also to Liane Morrissette (buy Zeitgeist the Canary now!) for contributing her Jones Soda induced sense of humour. Thanks to my sister Carmen for hanging on to her EZ Bake Oven for the past twenty years. Kim, thanks for putting up with the artist in me. Ruchi, thanks for keeping my antlers in shape. Oxana, thanks for the movie breaks. Finally to Pierre, mon chum, and Dale, my business partner: see you in SB.

First published in Canada by
McArthur & Company
322 King Street West, Suite 402, Toronto, Ontario, Canada M5V 1J2

Canadian Cataloguing in Publication Data

Tetro, Marc, 1960-
A Barbecue for Charlotte

ISBN 1-55278-112-7

I. Title

PS8589.E884B37 1999   jC813'.54   C99-931754-7
PZ7.T47Ba 1999

Printing and bindery: Friesen Printers

Printed in Canada

(FABULOUS!)

even THOUGH THEY were siSTers, everyone COULD TeLL THaT CHaRLOTTe anD TiFFanY were DiFFERenT.

and all the boys with antlers were playing volleyball.

How could she fit 'n?

CHARLOTTE TRIED TO GET HER ears TO STAND UP.

BUT THAT WAS DEFINITELY A FLOP.

no one could believe that she had a Barbecue on Her Head, But CharLotte FeLt Like a miLLion Bucks.

Who needed antLers?

She couLDn'T wait To Get Home!

"Hi mom,
Hi Grandma,
Hi Tiff!"

"I'm Home!"

"Hey Charlotte,
What's Cookin'?"
Teased Tiffany.

"Can't You See That's
a Barbecue on
Your Head?"

"WELL I LiKe iT!
WHY Can'T everYone
just Leave me
aLone?"
CrieD CHarLoTTe as
sHe ran
DownsTairs.

"Leave THiS To me",
saiD GrandMa.

"You know, Charlotte, you remind me of your mother when she was your age — she liked to try new things too... and that's OK."

"Besides, I like your new look!"

meanwhile, TiFFanY, STILL GiGGLinG at CHarLoTTe, WenT ouT To Pick some PreTTY FLowers.

"WELL, WELL, WELL," snarled the wolves, "what do we have here?"

THE WOLVES QUICKLY
SURROUNDED TIFFANY.
FROZEN WITH
FEAR, SHE DROPPED
HER BASKET OF
PANSIES.

Charlotte heard Tiffany's cries and came charging to the rescue.

THE WOLVES HAD NEVER
SEEN ANTLERS
LIKE THAT
BEFORE!

THEY
SCATTERED
BACK INTO THE FOREST.

Tiffany was so relieved
to see Charlotte.
"I thought I was a goner!
I'm sorry that I laughed
at you before, Charlotte."

"That's ok, Tiffany."

After all this excitement,
Charlotte and Tiffany
headed for home.

"GOOD NIGHT TIFFANY."
"GOOD NIGHT CHARLOTTE."